Robot at the Zoo

written by Pam Holden
illustrated by Richard Hoit

Robot went to the zoo
with his friend Charlie.

"What is that long animal
with spots?" asked Robot.

"That's called a snake,"
said Charlie.

"What's that animal with
a big nose?" asked Robot.

"That's called an elephant,"
said Charlie.

"What is that big animal
with horns?" asked Robot.

"We call that a rhino,"
said Charlie.

"What's that animal with black and white stripes?" asked Robot.

"That's called a zebra,"
said Charlie.

"What is that animal with
a long neck?" asked Robot.

"We call that a giraffe,"
said Charlie.

"What's that little animal
with a shell?" asked Robot.

"That's called a tortoise,"
said Charlie.

"What is that animal with
yellow ears?" asked Charlie.

"That's my dog," said Robot.
"Here are all my beautiful
animals!"